Get the Glue, Lew!

T0337136

Written by Jane Clarke

Illustrated by Rupert Van Wyk

Collins

Who and what is in this story?

Listen and say

castle

glue

Lew

Grandpa

Grandpa has got a present for Lew.
It's a kit to make a castle.

Lew and Grandpa can make it.
Lew says, "Wow! Thank you!"

5

There are lots of bits in the kit.
Grandpa says, "What do we do?"

There's one tool.

Lew says, "Look at this!"

They try to find the right bits.
Grandpa says, "Where is this?"

This bit fits, and that bit fits.

They've got the right bits. They haven't got the tool.

Lew says, "What do we do?"
Grandpa says, "Get the glue, Lew!"

Lew gets the glue.
Grandpa holds the bits.

Grandpa says, "Lots of glue, Lew!"

There's lots of glue on the castle.

There's lots of glue on Lew and Grandpa, too.

Grandpa and Lew like the castle.

The cat likes the castle, too!

The cat is in the castle!
Lew says, "Oh, no!"

Grandpa says, "I haven't got any glue, Lew."

Lew says, "I've got the right tool!"

The castle is a good present for Lew.

It's a good present for the cat, too!

Picture dictionary

Listen and repeat

bit

fit

kit

present

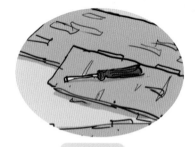

tool

1 Look and order the story

2 Listen and say

Collins

Published by Collins
An imprint of HarperCollins*Publishers*
Westerhill Road
Bishopbriggs
Glasgow
G64 2QT

HarperCollins*Publishers*
1st Floor, Watermarque Building
Ringsend Road
Dublin 4
Ireland

William Collins' dream of knowledge for all began with the publication of his first book in 1819.

A self-educated mill worker, he not only enriched millions of lives, but also founded a flourishing publishing house. Today, staying true to this spirit, Collins books are packed with inspiration, innovation and practical expertise. They place you at the centre of a world of possibility and give you exactly what you need to explore it.

© HarperCollins*Publishers* Limited 2020

10 9 8 7 6 5 4 3 2 1

ISBN 978-0-00-839750-0

Collins® and COBUILD® are registered trademarks of HarperCollins*Publishers* Limited

www.collins.co.uk/elt

British Library Cataloguing in Publication Data

A catalogue record for this publication is available from the British Library.

Author: Jane Clarke
Illustrator: Rupert Van Wyk (Beehive)
Series editor: Rebecca Adlard
Commissioning editor: Fiona Undrill
Publishing manager: Lisa Todd
Product managers: Jennifer Hall and Caroline Green
In-house editor: Alma Puts Keren
Project manager: Emily Hooton
Editor: Emma Wilkinson
Proofreaders: Natalie Murray and Michael Lamb
Cover designer: Kevin Robbins
Typesetter: 2Hoots Publishing Services Ltd
Audio produced by id audio, London
Reading guide author: Emma Wilkinson
Production controller: Rachel Weaver
Printed and bound by: GPS Group, Slovenia

MIX
Paper from
responsible sources

FSC
www.fsc.org
FSC™ C007454

This book is produced from independently certified FSC™ paper to ensure responsible forest management.

For more information visit: **www.harpercollins.co.uk/green**

Download the audio for this book and a reading guide for parents and teachers at www.collins.co.uk/839750